Brady Brady
and the Singing Tree

Written by Mary Shaw

Illustrated by Chuck Temple

Stoddart
Kids
TORONTO • NEW YORK

Visit www.templetoons.com for more Brady Brady information

Published in Canada in 2002 by
Stoddart Kids,
a division of Stoddart Publishing Co. Limited
895 Don Mills Road, 400-2 Park Centre, Toronto, Ontario M3C 1W3

Published in the United States in 2002 by
Stoddart Kids
a division of Stoddart Publishing Co. Limited
PMB 128, 4500 Witmer Estates, Niagara Falls, New York 14305-1386

www.stoddartkids.com

To order Stoddart Kids books please contact General Distribution Services
In Canada Tel. (416) 213-1919 FAX (416) 213-1917
Email cservice@genpub.com
In the United States Toll-free tel. 1-800-805-1083 Toll-free FAX 1-800-481-6207
Email gdsinc@genpub.com

06 05 04 03 02   2 3 4 5

National Library of Canada Cataloguing in Publication Data

Shaw, Mary, 1965–
Brady Brady and the singing tree

ISBN 0-7737-6272-8

1. Parent and child — Juvenile fiction. 2. Hockey — Juvenile fiction.
I. Temple, Chuck, 1962– II. Title.

PS8587.H3473B737 2002   jC813'.6   C2001-902928-4
PZ7.S534258Brs 2002

Parental pressure comes into play when a hockey dad takes the game too seriously.

THE CANADA COUNCIL | LE CONSEIL DES ARTS
FOR THE ARTS | DU CANADA
SINCE 1957 | DEPUIS 1957

*We acknowledge for their financial support of our
publishing program the Canada Council, the Ontario Arts
Council, and the Government of Canada through the
Book Publishing Industry Development Program (BPIDP).*

Printed and bound in China by Book Art Inc, Toronto

To Brad,
a wonderful hockey dad — but a horrible singer
Mary Shaw

To Kathy,
for being there.
Chuck Temple

Brady was worried. His friend Elwood hadn't been very happy lately, and Brady was pretty sure he knew why.

Ever since Elwood had lumbered into the dressing room, twice as tall as the other kids, the Icehogs had called him "Tree". Tree liked his nickname way better than "Elwood". And he loved to play hockey, just for the fun of it.

Tree's dad LOVED hockey, too, but for a different reason. He dreamed of Elwood becoming a big star one day and playing in the NHL. That seemed to be all that mattered to him. So, when Brady noticed that Tree was feeling down, it wasn't hard to figure out what was wrong.

Between games, Tree's dad always made him do sit-ups, push-ups, and laps. Tree hated running laps.

On the way to games, his dad talked hockey non-stop. Tree just wanted to listen to the radio.

Before games, while his friends played mini-sticks with a tapeball in the dressing room, Tree was usually with his dad. They sat in the stands watching other teams while his father pointed out what the players were doing right or wrong.

At games, Tree — and everyone else — could hear his dad yelling at him.

"Skate faster!" "Keep your head up!" "Wake up out there!"

It was embarrassing. Sometimes Tree wanted to take his equipment off and forget about playing altogether. Couldn't his dad see that he just wanted to play hockey for the FUN of it?

The Icehogs felt badly for Tree. Brady wanted to help, but he wasn't sure what to say. Then one day, he began to dream out loud as the Icehogs got dressed for a game. Pretty soon the rest of the team was dreaming too, even Tree.

"Wouldn't it be **great** to be a *woman* player in the NHL!" Tes exclaimed.

"Wouldn't it be **great** to get a *shutout* in the NHL!" chimed in Chester

"Wouldn't it be *great* to score a *hat trick* in the NHL!" Brady added.

"Wouldn't it be *great* to *sing* in the NHL!" shouted Tree.

*"**WHAT?!?!?!?!**"* Everyone froze.

"Did you say, *'**sing**'* in the NHL?" Brady asked.

"Yeah, Brady Brady," said Tree. "I've always wanted to sing the anthem at an NHL game. Don't tell my dad."

With all of the daydreaming going on,
the Icehogs had to rush their team cheer.

*"We've got the power,
We've got the might,
Tree wants to be a singer,
And that's all right!"*

The Icehogs dashed out of the dressing room and, without another word, pushed Tree to center ice. The crowd fell silent. Nobody knew what was going on, especially Tree.

"You don't need to tell your dad," Brady whispered in his ear. "Show him."

"Brady Brady, I ca . . ."

Tree was suddenly left standing alone. He closed his eyes, lifted his chin, opened his arms wide . . . and began to sing.

He had the most *incredible* voice!

When he was finished, the crowd clapped and whistled. Both teams slapped their sticks on the ice. There had never been so much noise in the building.

Tree grinned from ear to ear. He looked into the stands for his dad.

His father was *not* grinning from ear to ear.

On the way home, Tree was reminded that he was a hockey player, not a singer. "No son of mine is trading a hockey stick for a microphone," his dad said gruffly.

Tree swallowed hard. "I *love* hockey, Dad, and I *want* to play, but only if I can have fun. And only if I can sing at all the Icehogs games. The Coach already asked me, and I said yes."

Tree's father looked surprised. He started to object, but instead he said, "Well, if you feel that way I guess you may. But only if you work extra hard at practices."

Tree agreed, and they had a deal.

For a while everything was fine. Singing made Tree so happy that his hockey improved. This, of course, made his dad happy. Not only that, the Icehogs began to get a lot of attention, both on and off the ice. Everyone was talking about their great games and the kid who sang the anthem. Tree was even interviewed for the community paper.

Then one day, the Coach made a surprise announcement.
The Icehogs had been invited to skate between periods at
a real NHL game!!!

It was a dream come true — for everyone except Tree. For Tree it was more like a nightmare.

"My dad will think this is my big chance to be a hockey star," he told Brady. "What if I goof up in front of everybody and disappoint him?"

"You won't," said Brady. "Besides, we'll all be out there. You'll be fine!"

No matter what Brady said, Tree was terrified.

On the night of the skate,
the building was jammed with noisy
fans anxiously awaiting game time.
The Icehogs could hear the buzz and
excitement as they sat in their dressing room.

When a knock came on the door, they all jumped, especially Tree.

"They're ready for you!" the Coach announced.

"But we're not supposed to come out until the first period ends!" said Brady.

"We aren't, but Tree is," beamed the Coach. "I've been saving the best part till last. Tree is going to sing the opening anthem!"

Tree was stunned. He just stood there with his mouth hanging open.

"Well, what are you waiting for?" came a voice from behind. Tree turned to see his dad with a microphone in his hand. "I'll trade you this microphone for your stick. Son, you're the best anthem singer I know."

The noisy fans fell silent as the spotlight focused on center ice. Stepping into the glare, Tree closed his eyes, lifted his chin, opened his arms wide . . . and began to sing.

As Tree bowed to the cheering crowd, he saw the face of his biggest fan, pressed up against the glass — grinning from ear to ear.